When four young friends discover an herb fairy at the park, they are drawn into an adventure beyond their wildest dreams. The Old Man of the Forest has cast a terrible spell, locking up much of the plant magic in the world. The Herb Fairies turn to the children for help, and everyone discovers that the only way to restore the magic is by working together. By the end of this thirteen book series, readers become keepers of plant medicine magic.

Herb Fairies
Book One: Stellaria's Big Find

Written by Kimberly Gallagher
Illustrated by Swapan Debnath
Produced by John M. Gallagher

If you are not sure what a word means or how it is pronounced, check the glossary in the back of the book.

Special Thanks to my mom, Cheryl Delmonte, a fellow writer, who has always encouraged my love for the craft of weaving stories for others to enjoy.

Special Thanks to Maryann Gallagher Agostin, Hailey Gallagher, Rowan Gallagher, Rosalee de la Forêt, and the LearningHerbs community.

ISBN: 978-1514807132

Published by LearningHerbs.com, LLC, Shelton, WA.
LearningHerbs and Herb Fairies logos are registered trademarks of LearningHerbs.com, LLC.
Herb Fairies is a registered trademark of LearningHerbs.com, LLC.
First Amazon print-on-demand edition, July 2015. Published and printed in the U.S.A.

The Herb Fairies series is dedicated to the memory of
James Joseph Gallagher, Sr.

For Rowan and Hailey...

CHAPTER 1
Rowan's Surprise Gift

"Race you to that cabin!" ten-year-old Rowan yelled, taking off down the gravel path.

Twelve-year-old Sarah took off after him, her long, dark legs taking easy strides, keeping her beside him. Her tight, black curls bounced as she ran.

Camie and Hailey started running too, laughing and shouting, "Hey, wait up. You two are too fast." Rowan had promised to show them the original Butt Slide Hill and the girls could hardly wait. Camie and Hailey loved their messy slides down the Butt Slide Hill at wilderness school, but Rowan assured them that this one was even better.

"Oooooowwww!" Hailey's screams made all the kids stop and look back at her. She'd been running as fast as she could on her little five-year-old legs, but she couldn't keep up with the older kids and had tripped and fallen on the gravel. Everyone rushed back to her and helped her sit up. "Aaaahhhhh, I'm bleeding, I'm bleeding!" she screamed. Hailey's knees had been scraped up on the rocks. "I want Mama!"

"Mama's coming, Hailey," Rowan said. "She's just walking from the playground with the little kids."

When Hailey realized how far away her mom was, she started screaming, "Plantain! Get me some plantain!"

Rowan began to look around in the grass nearby. He was searching for the broad leaves with the parallel veins that both he and Hailey knew so well. It was great for bee stings, and would also stop the bleeding and clean out Hailey's scrapes. Unfortunately, it was still early March, and there was no plantain to be found. Rowan could hear Hailey crying even though Sarah had pulled her onto her lap and six-year-old Camie was singing Hailey's favorite silly songs. He hated it when his little sister was hurt and wanted to help, but he was about to give up. Then he spied a patch of chickweed growing beside one of the camping yurts, a big canvas tent on a wooden deck.

"I can't find any plantain," he called to Hailey, "but I'm bringing a bunch of chickweed." He ran over and picked a big handful, then went running back to Hailey, holding out the pile of chickweed.

"Ewwww," Sarah said when she saw the pile of chickweed in his hands. "What are you guys going to do with that?"

Hailey, however, stopped crying completely and her eyes lit up. "Rowan!" she shouted. "You found a fairy! You brought me a fairy!" Hailey was so excited, she jumped up and ran to her brother, forgetting all about her scraped knees.

"What?" said Rowan. "What are you talking about?"

"Right there, riding on the pile of chickweed! She must be the chickweed fairy. Look at her sparkly green dress. The bottom is even shaped like chickweed leaves, and she's got a sparkly chickweed hair clip in her hair. Oh, aren't her shoes cute! Camie, look. A fairy. A real fairy!"

Camie ran up beside her, smiling and laughing too. "I love the golden, glittery patterns on her wings," she said.

Rowan and Sarah shook their heads and blinked their eyes. They did not believe in fairies...until now. Rowan was so surprised to find the tiny being sitting delicately on top of the pile of chickweed that he almost dropped her.

"Can I hold her? Can I?" Hailey asked Rowan.

"I believe that's *my* choice," said the chickweed fairy. She spread her slender golden wings and flew lightly over to land on Hailey's hand. The chickweed fairy had thin arms and legs with sharp elbows and bony knees. She had straight blond hair like Camie's and captivating blue eyes. "My name is Stellaria," she said, "and I'm so glad I found you."

"You mean *you* were looking for *us*?" Sarah asked. "I thought we found you."

"Well, I was looking for some children who care for plants, and you four seem to fit that description. We've all been looking, for quite a while now, actually."

"All?" said Camie. "You mean there are more of you?"

"Oh, yes, lots! It's the herb fairies that have been trying to find you, though."

"The herb fairies! My parents are herbalists!" Hailey was delighted. "Why have you been trying to find us?"

"Maybe we should get that chickweed the boy found onto your scraped knees and then I'll tell you," said Stellaria.

It was only then that the kids realized they had all forgotten about Hailey's scraped knees. Rowan handed Hailey the chickweed and she quickly chewed it up and put the poultice she'd made onto her knees. Sarah grimaced a little when she saw what Hailey was doing. She didn't feel like it was the right time to protest about putting gooey green plant muck on a scrape. The poultice took the sting away immediately and stopped the little bit of bleeding.

"Now, why have you been searching for us?" asked Rowan.

"Well, ummmmm." Stellaria looked like she wanted to run away and hide rather than having all those big eyes looking down at her. She took a deep breath and looked down at the table when she spoke. "You see," she said quietly, wrapping her arms around herself, "well...oh, why did

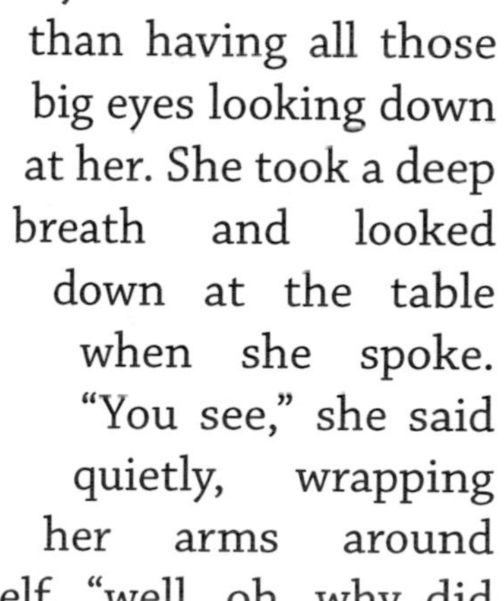

it have to be me who found you? I never thought it would be me..."

"You're a little shy, aren't you?" said Sarah kindly. "Would it help if we close our eyes?"

"Maybe," Stellaria admitted sheepishly.

The kids all closed their eyes to listen.

"We've noticed," Stellaria started tentatively, "we've noticed that lots of people are forgetting about how useful the plants are. They are forgetting about the magic that's in them. For a long time we didn't care. We loved the plants so much we just hid among them, enjoying their magic and their company. But now, it seems like our herb fairy magic is fading too. We had a big meeting, the fairies and the plants. The plants are very sad that humans have forgotten about how to use their medicine. They think if something isn't done even their magic might fade from the world forever."

"Oh no!" said Hailey, looking down at her knees. She thought about how sad she would be if she couldn't look to the plants when she needed healing help.

"What can we do?" said Rowan.

"You mean you want to help?" said Stellaria, looking up, her starry eyes filled with hope.

"Of course," said all of the children together. "But what should we do?"

"I really don't know," said the fairy. "We just thought it was important to find some children who know that the plants have magic, like you. That's about as far as we got with our plan, and we've been looking ever since."

Everyone was silent for a moment, thinking about what the fairy had said.

"I wish I could ask some of my fairy friends," said Stellaria quietly. "I know Dandy would have an idea. He always seems to come up with something."

"Could you take us with you to fairyland?" Hailey asked eagerly.

"We'd love to meet all the other fairies!" said Camie.

Stellaria sat down and cradled her face in her long, jointy fingers, thinking the idea over.

"Well, I suppose I could take you to the Fairy Herb Garden," she said finally. "Anyway, I'd love to show you my special chickweed patch home." She glowed when she spoke of her home, and the children guessed it must indeed be a pretty special place for her.

"Will you sprinkle us with fairy dust?" asked Hailey. She jumped up and down, her eyes shining.

"Indeed!" said Stellaria, taking a sparkling handful of fairy dust from her satchel. She flew over the top of the children and sprinkled them all.

As the dust settled gently atop their heads and on their skin the children felt a tingling sensation wash over their bodies. Then a gentle wind whirled around them and they found they were shrinking, but something more than that was happening. When the wind settled and they looked around, they were no longer anywhere near Butt Slide Hill.

CHAPTER 2
In the Fairy Herb Garden

All four children looked around in wonder. They were perched on the stem of a chickweed plant. The stem had silky hairs which kept them from sliding. They were surrounded by succulent, oval green leaves.

"You can really see how the hairs on the stems grow in a single row when you're this little," said Rowan.

"Oh, look at the pretty starry flowers!" Camie exclaimed. The white flowers were all around them, bringing a delicate, sweet beauty to Stellaria's chickweed home.

As the children looked around, they realized they were indeed in the fairy's home. There was a bed fashioned of twigs and lined with a mattress of cottonwood fluff. Two little chairs with flower seat cushions were pulled up to a carved wooden table. A cozy chickweed-stuffed couch faced out through an opening to the Fairy Herb Garden.

"Welcome," said Stellaria. "Would you like some elderberry juice?" Her eyes sparkled. She was enjoying the children's obvious delight.

"I've never had elderberry juice," said Sarah a little doubtfully.

"I'll have some," said Hailey. "I love the elderberry syrup my mom makes for our colds."

"I'll try some too," said Camie, a daredevil known for her crazy kitchen experiments.

"I'm afraid I don't have enough chairs for you all," Stellaria apologized. "Oh, but I do have a picnic blanket!"

She spread a blanket of woven grass out beside the table and they all sat down. She passed around nutshell cups full of dark purple liquid and gave them each a chickweed leaf to nibble on as well.

"This leaf is as big as my head," Hailey laughed, taking a bite. "I love chickweed," she said. "It's so delicious."

"Yes," agreed Stellaria, "and it's really good for you. It's full of vitamins and minerals, and it helps you get the most from all the other foods you eat as well." Stellaria's voice tinkled like gently ringing bells when she spoke about her plant.

"Really?" said Camie. "I've never even tried it."

"Me neither," said Sarah.

"Oh, our mom makes pesto out of chickweed, and we put it in our salads whenever we can find it," said Rowan. "It's one of her favorite plants, because both Hailey and I like it and she's always trying to get us to eat our greens."

"Wow," said Sarah. "This is really good, kind of juicy and a little bit sweet. Can I have another leaf?"

Stellaria laughed her tinkling laugh and waved her hand at the plant surrounding them. "Help yourself," she said. "The plants are so happy when you pick them and use their medicine. Just be sure and pick the leaves carefully. It's easy when you're small, but remember when you become big again. Always leave some leaves on the stems when you're picking chickweed, and leave the roots in the ground. Then the plant will continue to grow and you can come back and pick more another time."

Sarah and Hailey carefully picked another leaf for themselves. Hailey did one of her famous silly dances and sang, "Elderberry, chickweeeeed, elderberry chickweeeeeed, fairy, fairy, fairy." She hopped from foot to foot and wiggled her hips, smiling a silly, happy smile. Her long brown hair fell in front of her face as she tossed her head at the end.

"Stellaria," said Sarah, smiling at Hailey's antics, "can you take us to your fairy friends? I hope we can find a way to help you."

"Oh yes," said Stellaria. "I didn't know it would be so fun to have children visit my house. I almost forgot all about why I brought you here. Come with me." Stellaria led them out a little opening toward the back of the room.

Looking around, the children noticed that they had emerged into the shade of a weeping willow tree. Even though the leaves were enormous, bigger than them, they recognized their familiar lance-like shape and feathery veins. They loved playing fort under the weeping willow trees at the park.

A fairy fluttered over to join them. The children knew immediately that she must be the willow fairy. With her long, slender arms and legs she looked like she would love dancing in the wind just like her tree. She had Chinese facial features and dark, straight hair. She was definitely older than Stellaria, and when she spoke her voice was gentle, wise and whispery. "Why, Stellaria," she said. "Who have you brought to our garden?"

"Children!" said Stellaria, excitement ringing in her voice. "They've come to help us recover the magic."

"Aaahhhhh, beautiful," whispered Willow. "Welcome, children, and thank you for coming."

"You're welcome," said Sarah and Rowan together.

"Look, Hailey, I think she's a dancer. Isn't she beautiful?" Camie whispered to Hailey. Both girls loved to dance and they were often whispering together about their upcoming ballet recital. They were so excited about their sparkly new costumes.

"I thought we should look for Dandy. Maybe he'll have an idea of what to do now that we've found them," said Stellaria.

"Good idea," said Willow. "I saw him just a few minutes ago so I don't think he'll be far away."

The fairies and children stepped out from under the willow tree into the bright sunshine. Once their eyes adjusted, they stared in wonder at their surroundings. All sorts of herbs were beginning to emerge from the soil. Violet and crocus flowers were mixed among the sea of green before them. A few of the bolder and more curious fairies flew over right away and began asking questions. "Who are you? Can you help? What's your name?..." They all shared the golden wings with glittery spiral patterns, with one pair pointing upward and another downward, but the fairies were all different shapes and sizes. Their skin and hair and eyes and clothes were all different colors, and their body shapes were as varied as the plants surrounding them.

"I never thought about fairies having different colors of skin like humans," mused Sarah. Growing up in a small town in Washington state, most of her friends had white skin. It was fun to be around so much diversity.

Stellaria smiled. "We often keep the skin color and some features from the parts of the world our plants come from."

It wasn't long before Dandy himself joined the crowd. His bright yellow hair reminded Hailey of a dandelion flower.

His showy, yellow-gold wings were rippled and sparkled in the sunshine.

"Oooooo. He's cute!" whispered Sarah.

"I *knew* you would be the dandelion fairy," said Hailey.

Dandy smiled at Hailey, and dimples appeared on his cheeks. His bright blue eyes shone with joy and delight. "Children!" he exclaimed. "Who found them? Was it you, Stellaria?"

Stellaria smiled shyly and nodded her head.

"Will you introduce us to your new friends?" Dandy asked gently. More and more fairies were arriving as Dandy spoke. There was a hum of excitement in the crowd.

Stellaria let each child say their name. "They say they would like to help us," she said excitedly.

"Yes," said Rowan. "How can we help? We love the plants!"

"We don't want their magic to be lost!" said Hailey, looking down at her green, healing knees.

Suddenly, the ground began to shake beneath their feet. The fairies took off in fright, completely disappearing among the plants.

"Troll!" said Dandy, but he remained close to the children. Willow and Stellaria also stayed, but they were trembling.

"Do I smell children?" roared the troll. "Children in the fairy garden?"

"Hide," whispered Willow. "Quickly, back beneath my tree's branches."

The children followed her into the shade, hardly daring to breathe.

"Where are you, children?" said the troll in a pleading voice. "Please come out. I won't hurt you. I like children."

"She probably likes them for lunch," said Dandy. "The trolls are horrible creatures, always stomping on our plants. We have to run for our lives."

Rowan bravely peeked from between the willow leaves. Camie came to his side to peer out too, but Hailey stayed well back. She was trembling like the fairies, and Sarah put a protective arm around her. The troll was gigantic compared to them now. She had green skin and bulging eyes. Her nose and ears were huge, and the pointed tops of her ears curled downward. Her gnarled fingers clutched at her cane, which she leaned on heavily.

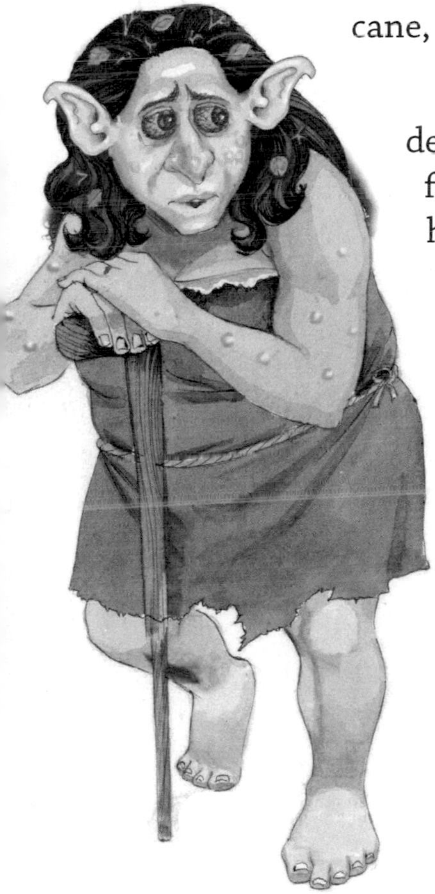

"Please come out," pled the troll in despair. "I've been waiting so long to find you, and I really do need your help."

CHAPTER 3
Troll Riddle

"Don't go out there, Rowan!" Hailey screamed.

But Rowan paid no attention. This troll would be no taller than his knees if he was full size, and Dandy's words had made him angry. Rowan was tall and stocky and he was used to standing up for himself. He sprang out, ready to punch and kick the troll and chase it away from the Fairy Herb Garden.

Camie caught his arm. "Wait, Rowan," she said. "Look at her. She is scary looking, but she has a kind face. Maybe she really does need help." Camie was smaller than Rowan, but she held on tight.

The troll swung her head around, searching for the source of Camie's voice. "Where are you?" she asked. "I can't see you."

"Down here!" Rowan shouted, his hands still curled into fists.

"Why, you're so small," said the troll in amazement, rubbing her red, bleary eyes.

"The fairy dust made us small when we came to the fairy garden," Sarah explained, stepping forward. "You said you needed our help?" she ventured to ask.

"Just look at me," said the troll. She motioned toward her wart-covered body and ran her hand along an open cut on her leg. "I think this is infected," she said dismally.

Camie turned her eyes away from the ugly gash, wrinkling her nose in disgust at the rotten smell of her. It was like the compost bucket at home when it had been sitting out too long. "What makes you think we can help?" she asked.

"You are the children, the ones who will help. The only ones who can help." The troll moved forward as she said this and reached out her hand.

"Look out, Camie!" Hailey screamed. "She's going to grab you!"

The troll sat back on her heels. "Grab you?" she repeated. Her brow wrinkled.

"Get off of those violets!" Dandy shouted, rushing forward angrily.

"AHHHHHHH! A fairy! A fairy!" The troll hid her face in her warty hands.

"Wait a minute," said Camie. "*You* are scared of *them*?"

"They are so mean. They yell at me and chase me out of the garden."

"Why do you stomp on our plants? You know our homes are in them," said Dandy. He glared at her, his hands on his hips.

The troll looked down at her feet. She saw the bent violet leaves and squashed purple flowers. Her eyes opened wide and she leaned over slowly, painfully. She reached down to smooth out the leaves and petals and straighten the little stems.

"Look," said Sarah kindly. "Here's a place where you can sit where there are no plants growing." She brought her into the shade of the willow tree, and the troll sat down, smiling gratefully.

Both Willow and Stellaria flew away quickly, hiding among the leaves of their respective plants. Willow, upset at having the troll in her special place, flew high up into the tree, getting as far away as possible. Stellaria was more curious and peeked out timidly from her chickweed home.

"I don't think she means any harm," said Camie. "Did you see how she looked at that plant? I don't think she even knew she was stepping on it or that you would be upset that she had."

"Hmpf!" said Dandy. "I just don't like trolls!" he said. "I don't trust them." With that he flew away, back out into the herb garden.

Now that Hailey could see the troll close up, she wasn't afraid anymore. She felt sorry for her, and stepped forward confidently with some chickweed in her hands. "This will help your leg," she said. "It just healed some scrapes on my knees."

Sarah and Camie looked in wonder at Hailey's knees. There was already fresh, pink skin over the scraped parts. "The chickweed did that?" Camie asked.

Hailey smiled. “Yep.”

“Wow,” said Rowan, “I’ve never seen the plants work so fast. Maybe it has to do with the magic of being in the Fairy Herb Garden.”

“It’s true,” came Stellaria’s tiny, tinkling voice. “The magic was stronger before, but it’s still working, speeding up the healing.”

“Stellaria, can we use some of your chickweed to make a poultice for the troll?” Hailey asked.

Stellaria forced herself to look at the cut, and when she did, her healing, compassionate nature came forward. She forgot, for the moment, her dislike of trolls. “Oh yes,” she said, and hurried over to her plant to pick some chickweed. She brought out her tiny mortar and pestle from inside her house and ground up the chickweed with a little water.

Hailey and Rowan stepped forward and put the chickweed poultice gently and carefully onto the troll’s wound. Camie had to look away. Seeing them tend the troll reminded her too much of all those days when her mom and dad were tending her sick sister. Even though the fever had finally broken, those had been the scariest days of Camie’s life.

“Aaah,” sighed the troll. “That feels cool. My leg was burning up.”

When the poultice felt warm to the touch, Hailey took it off and replaced it with a new poultice.

Sarah looked on in amazement. She would never have thought that mashed-up plants could help heal wounds. At home her mom always used Neosporin or Bactine when she had a cut.

Camie dared to look over when she heard the troll was feeling better, but she was still thinking about her sister. "Hey," she said, "we've been gone a long time. I wonder if Lizzy is missing me."

Stellaria spoke up. "Don't worry, Camie, time passes differently here in the Fairy Herb Garden. I can get you back before anyone misses you."

"What's your name?" Hailey asked the troll as she helped Rowan put the poultice on the wound.

The troll's eyes opened wide at that question and she looked around somewhat helplessly. "I don't remember," she said. Then as the chickweed began to pull the infection from the wound, the troll's head seemed to clear and she said, "That's it. That's why I was looking for you. I remember part of the riddle now."

"Riddle?" said Camie, giggling.

"Yes, the children must answer the riddle to guess your name." She said it as if she were repeating something she'd been told long ago.

"I love riddles!" said Sarah. "What do you remember?"

"Well, let's see. Let's see. My name is five letters long and begins and ends with the same letter." The troll paused for a moment and looked down at her leg. She squealed with delight when she saw how well it had healed.

"Is that it?" asked Sarah.

"No. No. There's more," said the troll with certainty. "The letter sounds like the name of a delicious, warm herbal drink." She closed her eyes and wrinkled her brow in concentration. "I know there's more, but that's all I can remember for now."

CHAPTER 4
Solving the Riddle

"Hmmmm," said Hailey. "A warm herbal drink? Chai?" That was her and Rowan's favorite warm herbal drink.

"No," said Rowan slowly. "That's not a letter. Let's see, A, B, C..."

All the children started going through the alphabet in their minds.

It was Sarah who got it. "T!" she said excitedly. "Tea is a warm herbal drink and a letter of the alphabet!"

"You're right!" said Rowan.

"So, her name begins and ends with T," said Camie.

"You're doing it. You're doing it. You're solving the riddle!" The excited troll started doing a little jig, causing her ears to flop up and down.

"Wow, your leg must really be feeling better," said Rowan, smiling. He noticed that the troll looked around as she danced to make sure that she didn't trample any more plants.

"Oh, if only I could remember the next part," she said. "But my eyes are so itchy and sore. I can't think straight."

Sarah looked at the troll's eyes. They were red and oozing a sort of white, creamy substance. "I think she's got pink eye," she said. "I had that once. It is miserable." There was compassion in her voice.

"I know my chickweed will help with that," said Stellaria in her delightful, tinkling fairy voice.

"It's a good thing you have such a huge patch of chickweed here, Stellaria," said Rowan. "We're using it up fast."

"There's still plenty," Stellaria assured him, and the children began gathering more leaves to make poultices for the troll's eyes. Soon they had the troll lying down with green, chickweed poultices over each eye.

"You know," said Rowan. "Chickweed poultices dissolve warts too. I've used them for that before."

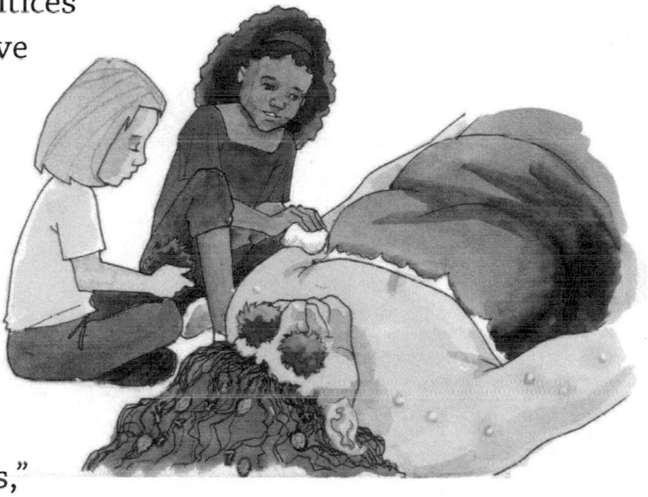

While the troll rested, the children made poultices for each of the troll's warts as well. "I can't believe I'm doing this," Sarah commented, remembering how disgusted she'd been when Hailey had chewed up the chickweed for her knees in the park.

"I know," said Camie. She didn't use plant medicine at home either. "It's pretty weird, but Hailey knows a lot about healing with plants."

"Yeah," Rowan agreed. "She's always helping Mom gather the plants and make the medicine at home."

The chickweed and fairy garden magic combined to shrink the warts and heal the pink eye in record time.

"Oh my," said the troll, sitting up. She blinked her eyes and looked down at her body. She hadn't been able to see anything clearly in so long, and to find her body free of those ugly warts was quite a surprise. She jumped straight to her feet and did her clumsy little dance of happiness. The children all laughed with delight, watching her.

"I remember something else!" she said.

"What? What is it?"

"You and us are part of my name."

"You and us? What does that mean?" said Hailey. "We're part of your name?"

"HaileyRowanSarahCamie?" said Sarah, laughing.

"I think we need another clue," said Rowan. "Can you remember anything else?"

The troll thought for a while, but then shook her head sadly. "No," she said, "my muscles are so sore. My whole body aches. That's all I can think about."

"We could make her a chickweed bath," said Hailey. "Sometimes my mom puts a chickweed infusion in my bath if my muscles are sore after one of my gymnastics practices."

"That's a good idea, Hailey," said Rowan, "but somehow I doubt she's going to fit in Stellaria's bathtub."

The children looked from Stellaria to the troll and back again, and laughed at the thought of that big troll trying to fit into a fairy bathtub.

"I have a bathtub at my house," said the troll. "Could we bring the chickweed there?"

"I knew it. I knew it!" Willow's voice came from the branches above. "She's trying to lure you to her house. Don't go with her," she warned. "Trolls can't be trusted!"

Stellaria did look very frightened at the thought of going to a troll's house, especially after Willow's warning.

"Oh, but we're so close to solving the riddle!" exclaimed Rowan.

"Is there anywhere else we could give her a bath?" Sarah asked the fairies.

Everyone thought hard, trying to think of a place where the troll could soak.

"There's the pond on the creek," said Stellaria, "but I'm afraid mixing the chickweed solution in a big pond would make it too weak to work."

"Maybe we could build a tub," said Rowan. He was always interested in building things. "We could carve one in a tree stump."

"That could take a long time," said Sarah, looking at the troll rubbing her arm and leg muscles.

Hailey looked into the now clear eyes of the troll. "I think we should go to her house!" she said. "Look at her. Without her warts and that wound and her eyes all healed, she's kind of pretty. I don't think she wants to hurt us."

"Me either," said Camie, coming up close. "I like her."

Sarah and Rowan looked at the little girls in surprise. Usually, they were scared of monsters. They too looked at the troll, and found that they didn't feel scared either. "That does seem like the easiest solution," said Rowan.

Stellaria gulped in alarm, but she helped them prepare the chickweed infusion. As it was steeping, Sarah noticed that Stellaria was trembling. "You're still scared about going to the troll's house, aren't you, Stellaria?" she said.

Stellaria nodded shyly. "We've been afraid of trolls for so long," she explained, "and I never go into the Enchanted Forest."

"You don't have to go, Stellaria," said Rowan. "We'll go with her and figure out the riddle and come back."

"The troll did say it was the children who would solve the riddle," Sarah reminded them all.

CHAPTER 5
In the Troll's House

So it was that the children set off with the troll, each carrying a jar of chickweed infusion. As soon as they left the Fairy Herb Garden, the landscape changed dramatically. When they entered the Enchanted Forest, they noticed that the plants around them no longer looked lush and healthy. Everything looked dry and wilted.

The children shuddered a bit. Since they were still fairy sized, the forest trees towered above them, and the Oregon grape bushes reminded them of holly trees at home. It was strange walking over fir needles that were half their height.

It was slow going, since they were so small, and the hunched-over troll moved so slowly with her painful muscles.

As they moved further from the Fairy Herb Garden, something strange began to happen. The children began to grow. Slowly, as they walked, they found themselves becoming taller and taller, until they were about the same height as the troll, about as tall as Rowan's ten-year-old human knees. That made the going much easier, and though they were still small, the forest seemed more familiar at this size.

Sarah was still feeling uncertain though. "Do you think we made the right choice?" she whispered to Rowan, looking around at the unhealthy forest. "I don't want to take the little ones into danger."

"I think it's going to be all right," Rowan said. "Hailey has really good intuition about people. I trust her judgment..."

"Come on, you guys!" called Camie over her shoulder. She and Hailey were following close behind the troll, holding hands and smiling.

It wasn't far to the troll's house. Soon they came to a small door built into the side of a hill. It reminded Hailey of the dugout house where Laura and Mary lived in the book *On the Banks of Plum Creek*. "Look, Rowan," she called. "It's just like Laura's house!"

Hailey's cheerful voice eased Sarah's fears. They all followed the troll inside. "Ugh!" said Hailey, holding her nose. The troll's house was not in good shape. Dirty dishes littered the table and sink. Clothes were strewn carelessly about the floor. A broken loom stood in one corner and colorful yarn was strewn carelessly about the room. The curtain that separated the bathtub from the rest of the room dangled at an odd angle, leaving the dirty tub exposed.

The children left the door open to let some of the stink escape.

The troll looked around, obviously ashamed. "I'm sorry it's such a mess," she said. "I just haven't been myself lately..." Her voice trailed off and she pulled out a chair and eased herself down into it. As she did, her eyes began to close, as if the day had been a bit too much for her.

"Well," said Rowan. "Let's get this bath going." He went over and straightened the little curtain, and began to wash out the tub. "The water is only cold," he said. "We'll have to heat some for the bath."

Sarah began gathering the dirty dishes. She found a teapot, but couldn't figure out how to work the stove.

"I think we need to build a fire in here," said Hailey, opening a door in the stove. "I remember seeing one like this in a movie once." The kids worked together to get a fire going. Luckily, Rowan had his flint and steel in his pocket. He'd taken it to the park that day in case they'd wanted to make a fire by one of the yurts. Before long, they had water heating up on the stove. Sarah used some of it to begin cleaning the dishes.

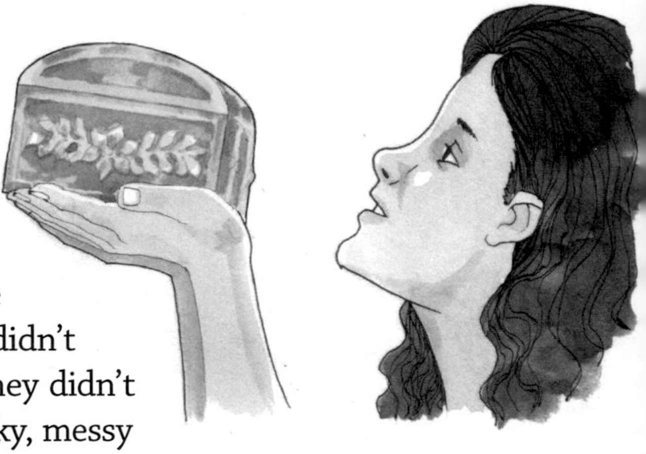

Camie and Hailey began rolling up the yarn that was scattered about and straightening the clothes on the floor. Usually they didn't like cleaning up, but they didn't like sitting in that stinky, messy place. In the end, they were rewarded for their work, because over by the troll's messy grass bed, under a worn nightshirt, they found a small, beautifully ornate golden chest. Unfortunately, it was tightly sealed and they could see no way to open it.

"Look!" shouted Hailey. Sarah stopped doing dishes and Rowan stopped preparing the bath to look over, and the troll woke up.

"Oh my," the troll said. "Did I fall asleep? I'm so sorry." She looked around the house in amazement. "Why, you've cleaned it up." Then her eyes fell on the chest that the children had found. "Would you look at that! I'd forgotten all about it. Isn't it beautiful?"

"Do you have the key?" asked Camie.

"What's in it?" asked Hailey.

"Well. I don't rightly know," said the troll, slowly rising to walk over to the chest. "Perhaps we'll find the key here somewhere." She began to look around aimlessly.

"Your bath is warm and ready now," said Rowan. "Perhaps we can look while you soak."

"Oh yes," said the troll, a smile spreading across her face. She disappeared behind the curtain and the children began to look around, but try as they might, no key appeared.

When the troll emerged from the bath, the children gave a gasp of amazement. She'd been completely transformed. She was no longer stooped over, though she was still short and stocky. She had put on a new dress, and without her sore muscles she moved easily and comfortably about her home. She'd even brushed out her curly brown hair, and her hazel eyes were clear and bright.

"I've remembered the last part of the riddle!" she announced.

"What is it?" Camie asked excitedly.

"I'm named after something all good friendships have at their core, something that is absolutely essential when sharing a secret."

"Hmmmm," said Sarah. All the children sat down on the floor in a circle to think. "It begins and ends with T," Sarah reminded them.

"And you and us are part of the name," said Rowan, still a bit mystified by that clue.

"What begins and ends with T?" said Hailey.

"T, T, Trot," said Camie. "Tent?"

"Those aren't things that are part of friendship, though," said Rowan.

"Love? Play?"

"Those don't start with T," said Hailey.

"I know! I know!" said Sarah.

"What is it?" asked Camie. "What?"

"Trust!" said Sarah. "You have to trust someone if you're going to tell a secret, and it begins and ends with T and it has the letter U and the word US in it!"

"You're right!" said Rowan, with excitement. "Is that it? Is your name Trust?"

"Yes!" exclaimed the troll. "Yes it is!" She did her little dance again. She was so happy.

CHAPTER 6
Magic Returned

Camie turned when she heard a tiny tapping on the window of the cottage. There was Stellaria, waving to her. Camie reached over and opened the window so the fairy could fly through.

"I'm so glad you're all okay," Stellaria said in a rush. "I was so worried about you. I had to come see..." Her voice trailed off as her eyes fell on the healed troll. "Wow," she said, "you look...you look beautiful."

Trust smiled and looked down at herself a bit self-consciously.

"Stellaria," said Rowan, "we'd like to introduce you to Trust. We solved the riddle and now we know her name!"

"Trust," repeated Stellaria quietly.

"And look what we found!" said Hailey, holding up the golden chest. "We've been trying to find a key, but we don't even really see a keyhole."

Stellaria ran her hand over the chest. "I think my magic, the chickweed magic, is inside," she said excitedly. "Trust, do you know how to open it?"

"I think perhaps we will all have to work together to do that," said the troll. "Yes, that's why you kids couldn't find a key. The way into the chest is through my weaving."

"Your weaving?" asked Camie.

"Yes, we must weave together, all of us." She was excited now, and began pulling out some of the balls of yarn that Camie and Hailey had rolled up for her. She also pulled out a small loom from inside a cabinet. Unlike the larger broken loom, this one was in perfect condition.

"Um, I don't know how to weave," said Sarah. She frowned and bit her lip.

"Oh, don't worry about that," said Trust. "This is a magic loom. You need only think what you want to add to the picture, choose your color and touch the loom. Here, I'll begin." She chose a beautiful blue, and as she touched the yarn to the loom a lake appeared on the cloth. "Add something that makes you happy," Trust instructed.

Stellaria flew forward with white yarn, and chickweed flowers appeared around the lake. Camie stepped forward with the yellow yarn, and wildflowers joined the chickweed flowers. Rowan chose a brownish red, and a hawk appeared in the sky above the lake. Sarah chose a yellow-orange so that the sun spilled down over the lake. Hailey picked a multicolored yarn and when she touched the loom fairies appeared among the wildflowers. With that final touch the

weaving shimmered and sparkled and disappeared as it released its magic.

The chest sprang open, and the children watched in amazement as a swirl of glittery green light whooshed from the box, spiraling in the air and spreading the fresh scent of chickweed throughout the troll's home. Then it rushed in a great stream through the open door and out into the world.

"The chickweed magic!" gasped Stellaria, tears of joy in her eyes. "We've returned it to the world." The tiny fairy glowed with glittering, green light. Her quiet, gentle strength shone in her sparkling eyes.

The children all hugged one another in delight, and before they knew it, more fairies were fluttering through the door and turning happy somersaults in the air. The children recognized Dandy and Willow among them.

When everyone settled down, they all looked at Trust and began talking at once. Sarah formally introduced Trust to the fairies and they all quieted to hear her story.

"But wait," said Stellaria, "if I don't get these children back to the park, their parents are going to start missing them."

"How long have we been gone in real time?" asked Rowan.

"Do we have to go?" asked Hailey.

"You better go at once," said Dandy, "but don't worry, we'll come find you again when we need more help in the Fairy Herb Garden."

"Wait," said Trust, looking down into the golden chest. From inside she pulled out four copies of the weaving they had made together. She presented one to each of the children.

Hailey had tears in her eyes as the little chickweed fairy flew above them, sprinkling fairy dust over them all. She clutched her weaving tightly. She had loved her adventure in the Fairy Herb Garden, and knew she would miss her new fairy and troll friends. But at least she knew now that she would be coming back to see them.

Back in the park, Hailey, Camie, Rowan, and Sarah looked around and down at themselves and their magical weavings. They blinked and hugged each other. Now it felt strange to be so big.

"Did that all really just happen?" Rowan asked.

The girls nodded at him, big smiles on their faces.

"It's a good thing we were all there," said Sarah, "or I'd never believe it was real."

"Rowan? Hailey? Where are you?" It was their mom, calling from the path where Hailey had fallen.

The kids came out from behind the yurt and ran to rejoin their parents, each carrying a magical reminder of their adventure together.

Glossary

Infusion (in-FEW-shun) A medicinal strength tea, often prepared using one ounce of dried herbs per quart of water and steeped for at least four hours.

Poultice (POLE-tis) A moist mass of plant material applied to the body to aid in healing.

Stellaria (Stel-AR-ee-a) Name of the chickweed fairy and also the scientific genus name of the chickweed plant.

What's Next?

Learn more about chickweed on HerbFairies.com! After you complete the Magic Keeper's Journal, color Stellaria, make some recipes, and print out a picture of her for your wall. Learn lots more about chickweed in Herbal Roots Zine, which has recipes, puzzles, activities, stories, songs and more!

Magic Keeper's Journal

Who's next? Meet...

Viola is the Violet Fairy. Join her in
Book Two: Secrets in the Scotch Broom.

Herb Fairies

Author Kimberly Gallagher, M.Ed. is also creator of *Wildcraft!, An Herbal Adventure Game*, by LearningHerbs.com. Her Masters in Education is from Antioch University in Seattle, and she taught at alternative schools in the Puget Sound region. Kimberly has extensive training in non-violent communication and conflict resolution. Her love of nature, writing, teaching, gardening, herbs, fantasy books and storytelling led her to create Herb Fairies.

Read the entire Herb Fairies adventure on HerbFairies.com!